HITCHHIKER'S GUIDE TO TREKKING IN UTTARAKHAND

DR ANSHUMALI PANDEY

ISBN 979-888629321-0

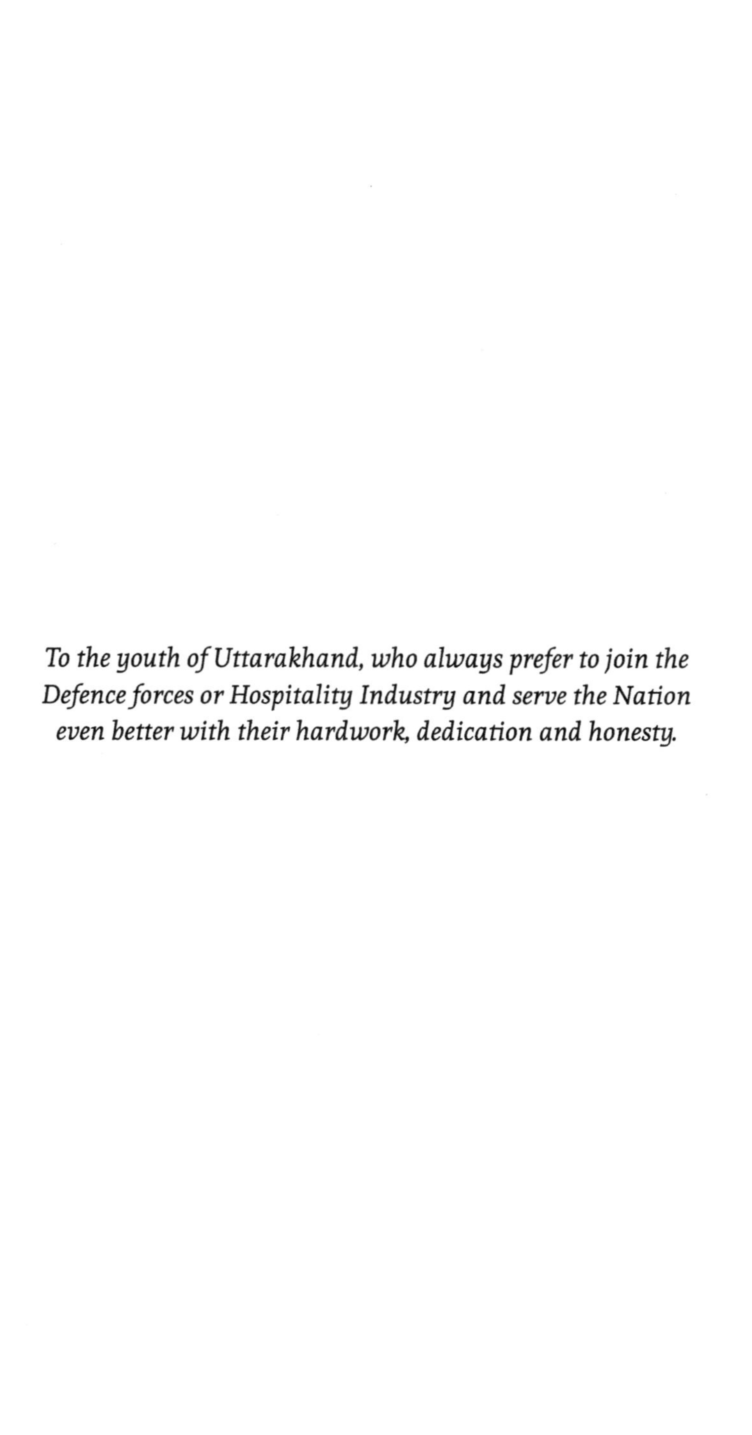

To the youth of Uttarakhand, who always prefer to join the Defence forces or Hospitality Industry and serve the Nation even better with their hardwork, dedication and honesty.

Contents

Contents

FOREWORD

Mr. Rachit Kumar, (Director – Gardenia Hotel, Spa & Resort, Haridwar; CEO – Hotel Ganges Rivera, Haridwar; Member of USBA, Uttarakhand; Member of CAOH (BCCI); Partner in Kumar Realtors.)

I am elated that Dr Anshumali Pandey, himself decided to write this Guide on Trekking in Uttarakhand after being an avid trekker himself in all of India. I myself belong to this beautiful state and will vouch for everything written in the book.

From thrilling mountain climbing to relaxing leisure walk, each single activity is delightful and worthy to time spending. Hill stations are visited by honeymooners to spend romantic time together, corporate people to take a break, traveller to enjoy the beauteousness of nature, family to enjoy vacation and creative persons to enhance their creativity level with fresh ideas.

Any Uttarakhand Hill station is a compilation of several popular destinations of Uttarakhand which are popular with the masses and have frequented visitors.

Don't search reasons for planning a holiday in the hill stations of Uttarakhand, simply pack your bags to take pleasure in the pristine scenery of the Himalayas.

Welcome to Uttarakhand with this book in your Backpack.

I

INTRODUCTION

Bordered by Tibet in the north, Nepal in the east, Himachal Pradesh in the west and the Gangetic plains in the south, Uttarakhand, the land of spirituality seems to be a jewel on the crown of Indian Territory. Being the originating point of significant Indian rivers, Uttarakhand is the abode of some of the best hill stations in north India. While the winter season can offer you the best views of snow packed mountain ranges, the same ranges can be the comfort zones in the scorching summer.

From thrilling mountain climbing to relaxing leisure walk, each single activity is delightful and worthy to time spending. Hill stations are visited by honeymooners to spend romantic time together, corporate people to take a break, traveler to enjoy the beauteousness of nature, family to enjoy vacation and creative persons to enhance their creativity level with fresh ideas. An Uttarakhand Hill station is a compilation of several popular destinations of Uttarakhand which are popular with the masses and have frequented visitors. Don't search reasons for planning a holiday in the hill stations of Uttarakhand and simply pack your bags to take pleasure in the pristine scenery of the Himalayas.

Uttarakhand is a 'paradise' for nature lover's and adventure sports like river rafting, trekking, paragliding, Corbett jungle Jeep safari, enthusiasts. Mussoorie, the 'Queen of Hills'; Nainital, Almora, Ranikhet, Pithoragarh, Pauri and Munsiyari are just few highlights for the nature lovers. For adventure and excitement, one may choose Mountaineering (Bhagirathi, Chowkhamba, Nanda Devi Kamet, Pindari, Sahastrataal, Milam, Kafni, Khatling, Gaumukh), Trekking, Skiing (Auli, Dayara Bugyal, Munsiyari, Mundali), Skating, Water Sports like rafting, boating and angling and Aero Sports like Hand Gliding, Paragliding (Pithoragarh, Jolly Grant, Pauri).Trekking adventure in the Uttarakhand's enchanting Himalayas have always been appealing the trekking lovers and adventure sports enthusiasts. Explore Valley of Flowers, Chopta and the beauty of Kumaon and Garhwal Himalayas.

II

TREKKING

Trekking is combination of hiking and walking activity in which people take multi-days trips in rural, under developed area. In another words, Trekking is making a journey / trip on foot, especially to hike through mountainous areas often for multiple days and along lovely mountains villages and enjoying nature and/or close contact with people in remote mountain villages where lifestyle sometimes is unchanged since many generations.

Trekking is also done in risky mountain areas so it will help to gain more adventurous build up capacity to the trekkers'. Trekker will get knowledge that is more adventurous with the real life scenario in mountain areas or in remote area. To be a trekker they must have to there things that are Budget, Holiday, willing to do adventure.

Trekking will not done free by the Trekking company so that they most pay the expenses during their trekking trip and They must have a holiday for such trip and last one is trekker must be capable to do a trek and he/she have to willing do adventure work. If people have all these attributes, they can easily do trek with contacting in our company, we will help to you people giving quality services according to clients desire.

There are two Types of Trek...

1. Camping Trek

2. Tea House Trek

1. Camping Trek:

Camping trek is little sophisticated trek than trek house trek because in Camping trek, Trekking organizer or we will carry the all things required for trek from Kathmandu or that places where all the necessary items are available. All things (all food items and Tent for sleep) will be always with the trekker during trek trips. Trekking will sleep in the tents and their staff (if any). Their staff will prepare meals as per in the menu provided in advance.

2. Tea House Trek:

Tea hose trek means doing trek by eating and sleeping at Tea/ guesthouse where the Teahouse are available for sleep and already setup by the villager for providing the service to the clients. Every day trekker will get the tea house to eat and sleep. In comparison to camping trek, teahouse trek is little cheep. But both trek are done in the same place only different is that camping trekker's get own prepare food by own office cook where as teahouse trekker's will get to eat food which prepared by tea house's staff.

Trekking can be done anywhere in the world. Certain areas are particularly popular with trekkers, including mountainous regions such as the Himalayas in Asia and the

Andes in South America. Treks also have been organized in other less-visited areas on almost every continent. Trekking destinations high altitude will be depends on the trekking destination chosen by clients.

III

STYLES OF TREKKING

There are three main 'styles' of trekking, each of which has pros and cons, but your choice will depend on your destination, budget, time available and personal preferences.There is no better or worse style, in fact you might find yourself combining styles in some destinations to provide a broader experience.

1. Independent trekking without a Guide:

For many, the idea of finding one's own way and living off the land is what trekking is all about. To be completely free to plan your day, to have all your gear on your back, and to interact one-on-one with locals is a liberating experience. Due to the nature of independent trekking it is normally a good idea to trek with a friend or in a small group of up to four for safety – larger groups tend to find it difficult to find accommodation.

Being an independent trekker doesn't mean to say that you cannot have a porter or a porter/guide. The introduction of the TIMS (Trekkers Information Management System) has made this option a little more complicated, but it is still possible to employ a local for almost any period of time, which can make tricky navigation and strenuous sections considerably easier. Most independent trekkers prefer to trek the main routes of the Annapurna, Everest, Langtang, Makalu, Manaslu, Mustang, Rolwaling and Tamang Heritage Trail areas as they offer teahouse accommodation and a standardised menu.

Trails in these areas are well marked and some of the local people speak enough of a range of languages that the individual trekker can get along with the most basic Nepali. Even though you may walk on your own, or with a local porter, it is in fact very rare that you will find yourself without company, especially in the evenings when you sit in the teahouse communal dining room.

The main trails are normally busy with local traffic so if you carry a pocket guide and map it is unlikely that you'll take a serious wrong turn, although getting a little lost is almost inevitable.Independent trekking is also the cheapest way to explore the mountains so it is popular with budget-conscious travellers.

There are a few drawbacks to independent trekking: coping with altitude and health problems on your own, logistical challenges, communication issues and safety concerns. None of these is insurmountable but they do need to be taken seriously both before and during your trek.

Altitude and health problems are best monitored and dealt with as part of a 'buddy system' – that is, you and your trekking companion look after each other (for more details, see Altitude Sickness, pp67-8).

There are also some potential logistical issues in high season: the most common is that many teahouses are booked in advance by organised trekking groups and you may find getting a room, or even floor space to sleep on, difficult and/or expensive.

If this is going to be your first visit to the Himalaya the independent option probably isn't the best style to kick off your adventures, unless you are the ultimate intrepid traveller and you stay on the main trails.

Independent trekking in remote wilderness areas is only suited to trekkers who have already learnt how their body deals with altitude, developed some familiarity with Nepali and the various customs of mountain communities, and have a good knowledge of Himalayan terrain and navigation.

2. *Teahouse trekking with a Guide:*

Recent years have seen a dramatic increase in both the number and the standard of facilities in villages on the main trails. For example, Namche in the Everest Region now boasts 24-hour electricity, a laundrette, multiple internet cafés, bakeries, and all the trappings of Thamel (the tourist district in Kathmandu) but at 3500m.

It is no surprise therefore that teahouse trekking with a guide has become incredibly popular. The convenience of teahouse trekking in the Everest, Annapurna and Langtang areas is a major drawcard for tens of thousands of trekkers every year. The subsequent level of investment by local communities in these regions is extraordinary compared to the level of poverty elsewhere in the Himalaya. Large teahouses with comfortable communal dining rooms, private bedrooms (some with en suite bathrooms) with mattresses and bedding, extensive menus or specialty restaurants and bakeries can make your trek a very comfortable experience.

Commercial trekking companies from all over the world sell organised walking holidays using these teahouses and a local guide agency, and they're flexible enough to suit almost any fitness and experience level. The role of a guide can encompass a great many activities. Apart from being the person who escorts you along the trail, they can often explain customs, culture, history, flora and fauna. A guide may also manage any porters (should you only want to carry a small pack), ensure your accommodation is booked, transport is confirmed, and that the food is well prepared; in fact your guide will probably become your personal assistant, man-Friday, guardian, and best friend. For this reason most good guides are normally snapped up by the bigger agencies and accompany groups booked by overseas trekking companies.

There are no major drawbacks to this style of trekking. However, there are a few issues that people regularly complain about. One is that teahouses that accept larger groups can be very noisy at night; for most people it's tougher to sleep at altitude, so anything that disrupts sleep is irritating. Another involves the decisions that your guide makes without consultation, like where to stay, or route options. Make sure you have a clear understanding of who makes which decisions. Small groups trekking with a guide may find it difficult to secure rooms or even meals in some teahouses that devote themselves to larger, more profitable parties.

If you are a woman trekking alone with a guide be aware that even simple acts can be misconstrued as a proposition.Booking a trek through an overseas operator means you don't get to have any choice of guide, but you do have the reassurance that they are probably going to be excellent and if not, you have recourse to complain.

The size of group you will be trekking with becomes important when you choose a 'packaged trek'. Some companies are still in the habit of sending over twenty trekkers into the hills with a single guide and a few porters, which is irresponsible and doesn't make for a good holiday.

The safety and security of local knowledge should not be underestimated, nor should the ability to communicate to your heart's content through your guide's interpreting. Finally, the chance to build a friendship with someone is perhaps the most remembered feature of any trekking holiday.

A group size of twelve to fourteen is normally considered a manageable maximum and you'll still get the opportunity to chat with your guide and spend time with any crew that they might hire.

One main advantage of hiring your own guide and teahouse trekking is that you can control your costs and stay within a budget that would be considerably less than booking with a big travel company.

The logistical convenience of having someone with local knowledge handling routine details such as where to stay, negotiating prices, and giving route directions is a great peace of mind.

3. Trekking with a camping crew:

The most flexible, comfortable and hygienic way to explore the Himalaya is on a camping trek. To have unrestricted access to trails, viewpoints, and passes you need to be self-sufficient, with the support of a team of experienced staff. For many trekkers their first trip to Nepal will be teahouse based, but the lure of what lies beyond the main trails is so strong they return for a camping trek, often to the more remote areas.

Trekking in Nepal was initially exclusively camping based so there is a substantial experience pool that means even the first-time camper will be comfortable and well looked after. Each morning you will be woken with a mug of tea delivered by a smiling sherpa (as opposed to Sherpas, the famous ethnic group from the Everest Region, see box p135), followed by a bowl of water to wash your face. Breakfast is preferably served al fresco in the morning sun as your crew packs up the camp. At some point along the day's trail your cook will have prepared a lunch for you at a scenic spot before you complete your journey to the next campsite and an extensive dinner menu.Shower, toilet and dining tents with tables and chairs complete your campsite and comfort comes courtesy of a foam mattress and pillow (usually an optional extra.

Nearly all remote or exploratory treks will be camping based as a group needs to have Sherpa and crew available to help cross passes and break trail. The roles of various crew members is normally well defined: the guide (or sirdar) is in charge; the sherpas look after clients on the trail, serve meals and make/break camp; the cook and kitchen staff prepare meals and wash dishes for the group, while the porters carry everything.

Normally, a guide discourages trekkers from becoming too friendly with the crew as companies are paranoid they might lose your future business to prospecting staff. With the increasing popularity of teahouse trekking, companies that specialise in camping treks are becoming more competitive so it is important to check the details of your trek before you depart.

The two most common ways companies cut costs are: firstly, increasing the amount of load the porters carry and not providing them with necessary clothing and equipment (see the International Porter Protection Group, www.ippg.net for how you should care for your porters and your obligations towards them); secondly, either the agency or the cook reduces the money dedicated to your food and fuel allowance.

It is important that the group leader should keep an eye on the quantity and quality of stocks. The obvious drawbacks to camping-style treks are perceived inconvenience and potentially having to share a tent with someone you would rather not sleep next to. To resolve both issues research is necessary.

Camping really is more convenient than teahouses on the condition that you have a slightly flexible itinerary, so you can ensure washing and relaxing time for all, especially when the weather is good. Almost all camping groups offer single occupancy tents but you normally have to specify when you book, and you should always check the terms and conditions.

For many, these drawbacks are easily mitigated and, in fact, are overwhelmed by the advantages of camping-style treks. Choosing your own path and rest spots offers a level of itinerary customisation that not even teahouses in the most popular regions can compete with.

The main benefit, however, is being able to explore remoter regions away from the main trails and meet some of the inhabitants of the wild Himalaya. It is hard to believe that there are still many villagers who have never seen a tourist, where communities greet you as an honoured guest and not as an opportunity to make another buck.

For many trekkers and trek leaders, camping-style treks are their favourite method of exploring Nepal; they often say that their experience feels more genuine. Camping brings you closer to nature, and the camaraderie built around a campfire often outlasts that of a teahouse trek.

Away from the main routes is where you'll most likely see many of the species for which the Himalaya is famous: red panda, black bear, musk deer, snow leopard and a multitude of birds.

Part A: Trekking in Garhwal

The Garhwal is one of the frequently visited areas in the Himalayas. The two river outlets of Ganga and Yamuna provide the main enterance to Garhwal Himalaya, throug the towns of Haridwar, Rishikesh, Dehradun ad Mussoorie. The Gangotri area near the source of the Bhagirathi River is the most popular destination for trakkers and mountaineers.

It is the gateway to many famous glaciers and spectacular peaks, apart from being one of the most sacred places in Garhwal. Two other important areas are Valley of Flowers and Badrinath, near the source of the Alaknanda River source are also much frequented.

The whole of Garhwal Himalaya is pilgrimage country, visited by thousands of travelers men ad women, yong and old, rich and poor, coming from every corner of India. It lies between the Punjab to the West and the Nepal Himalayas to the East. This is one area in the Himalayas, which has something to offer to all the mountaineers, the trekkers, the naturalist and the photographer. As Garhwal houses some of the holiest of Hindu shrines, it attracts millions of pilgrims every year from all over the Indian sub-continent.

The Garhwal Himalayas have attracted mountaineers from all over the world, to attempt and scale the mighty peaks in this region. A Garhwal trekking tour in this area, combined with visits to the holy temples of Gangotri,

Kedarnath, Badrinath and Yamunotri, will add spiritual experience of the Himalayas as you watch the stream of people bathing and lining up in front of the temples to have a view of holy shrine, and to wash away, the sins of a lifetime.

IV

Deharadun Mussorie Trek

Dehradun Mussoorie in Indian States of Uttarakhand, like other hill resorts in India, came into existence in the 1820s or there abouts, when the families of British colonials began making for the hills in order to escape the scorching heat of the plains. Small settlements grew into large stations and were soon vying with each other for the title of "queen of the hills." Mussoorie's name derives from the Mansur shrub (Cororiana nepalensis), common in the Himalayan foothills; but many of the house names derive from the native places of those who first built and lived in them.

V

Dodi Tal Trek

High up in the mountains is the Dodi tal lake- mysterious, alluring, and simply beautiful! The serene, tranquil surroundings, gurgling streams, crystal clear water, and dense alpine forests make for an ideal retreat. The trek from Dodital to Yamnotri takes you through high altitude grasslands and dense virgin forests. The scenery en-route is really astounding! The trek for Dodi Tal commences from Uttarkashi or Kalyani, which can be approached by motor. Kalyani to Agoda is a gradual climb through woods, fields and villages along· a mule track. The trek from Agoda to Dodi Tal is steep and through thick forests.

VI

Gangotri Nandanvan Trek

Celebrated in Hindu mythology and religion, the Garhwal Himalayas are said to be the "Abode of the Gods". The river Ganges takes its source in this remote massif, at the sacred shrine of Gangotri, and rushes down to the plains in a torrential fury. Very few trekkers follow this itinerary which will lead to one of the most important spots of Hindu spirituality, where you will experience a strange atmosphere of religious fervour.

From Kedarnath, where hundreds of pilgrims arrive from all regions of India, the path proceeds at first along the sacred Bhagirathi river, then through dense forests and grassy areas as far as Lata. From there it is a 5-hour drive to Gangotri, where the second part of the trek starts.

Near Gaumukh, close to the Source of the Ganges, you will experience the strange view of half-naked saddhus in the lotus position, meditating on the bank of the bubbling stream pouring out the glacier. Further up, Tapovan is a grassy area with numerous brooks, surrounded by snowy peaks. It is a round-trip itinerary starting in Kedarnath, along the sacred Baghirathi river, then heading west, through dense forests and grassy areas. The northern part of the itinerary will offer magnificent views of several high altitude lakes.

VII
Tons Valley Trek

A trek in around Tons Valley is most westerly inlet of Garhwal Himalaya. The Dhauladhar Range separates it from the Baspa Valley of Kinnaur in Himachal Pradesh. Passes over this range are comparatively new trekking experiences for visitors because the whole of kinnaur has been a restricted area until the 1990s. Har Ki Dun has long been a popular destination, at the upper NE end of the Tons, near the junction of three small glaciated valleys. Below this point other side valleys offer attractive hiking. Access is by bus from Mussorie or Dehradun to Netwar (1380m) and Sankri. You will also find here representatives of the Himalaya Trekking Association, which is supposed to be an authorized government agency.

VIII

Har Ki Dun Trek

The Har Ki Dun Trek or Har Ki Doon Trek is an ideal trek for first time and experienced trekkers. The journey is scenic, is not too hard while being in no way "easy" and the pay-off of the scenery at Har Ki Dun Valley is a great payoff for the effort.The trek to Har Ki Dun is one of the most scenic treks a person with no prior trekking experience could ask for. The Har Ki Dun Valley is known for its wild flower meadows and the birdlife as it falls in the boundaries of the Govind National Park. Har Ki Dunhas great views of the Hata and Swargarohini peaks along with Har Ki Dun peak of course. On the way you can see Bandarpuchh and Black Peak in the distance. Har Ki Dun's alpine flowers and its rich green landscapes with enough steep climbs and level walks – are sure to interest any trekking enthusiast or nature lover.

IX

Kauri Pass Trekking

A straightforward trip offering glorious view of some of the highest mountains of Garhwal Himalaya. The Kauri pass trek is amongst the best in the Garhwal Mountains. The trail takes you through lush green fields, remote villages and virgin forests. Lord Curzon, once the viceroy of India, traveled this route, hence it is also known as Curzon's Trail. Ghat, 19km SE of Nand Prayag, is the starting point. This small town on the main Rishikesh-Joshimath road at the junction of the Mandakini and Alaknanda rivers has tourist and forest rest houses, PWD bunglow and rest house. Best Period: June and September-October.

X

Nanda Devi Treks

This classic trek takes us across the picturesque meadows and valleys that border the western edge of the Nanda Devi Sanctuary. Situated in the upper watershed of the Alaknanda River in the Garhwal Himalaya, Nanda Devi Sanctuary is a vast glacial basin segmented by a series of parallel ridges emanating from the encircling mountain ramparts. The sanctuary is a vast amphitheatre some 132 km in circumference encompassing some of the most formidable gorges and covering about 625 sq. km of snow and ice.

The most important ridge is the Rishikot-Devistan ridge which separates the inner sanctuary from the basin. The sanctuary is encircled by high mountain ranges and is accessible only from NW for a short period. The mountain ranges and is accessible only from NW for a short period. The mountain rim has such high peaks as Dunagiri 7066m, Changabang 6864m, Kalanka 6931m, Rishi Pahar 6992m, Nanda Devi East 7434m, Nanda Khat 6611m, Trisul 7120m.

Nanda Devi main 7816m is situated on a short ridge projecting from eastern rim at Nanda Devi East. This amazing feat of endurance and determination was capped when Tilman later returned to conquer the peak itself.

Sadly, the mystic of the area led to an excess of expeditions and ecological damage and the Sanctuary was closed in the 1980's. Investigations are currently underway to assess the recovery. Understandably, the country that surrounds the Sanctuary now has its own attractions for walkers and pilgrims alike. The immediate landscape has been beautifully tamed by centuries of low-key habitation and cultivation but the constant backdrop of the mighty Himalayan peaks makes for a magnificence unrivalled elsewhere in the region.

XI
Roopkund Trek

Roopkund is a magnificent tourist spot located in the Himalayas. Roopkund Lake is well-known as Mystery Lake; this lake was jam-packed with skeletons and bones of human being due to a disaster that happened here around 14th century. Set in Himalayas at an altitude of about 16,499 feet, it is totally uninhabited. The glacial lake is situated on a significant pilgrimage route to Nanda Devi Cult where the famous Nanda Devi Raj festival is held once in every 12 years. Trekking through, one comes across virgin forests, bubbling streams, temples, snow and Himalayan peaks Bedni Bugyal and Trisul. Trekkers start from Lohajung, climb to a hillock at Wan to reach Ran ki Dhar, then to Bhaguwagasa to finally arrive at Roopkund.

XII

Chopta - Chandrashila Trek

The Chopta Chandrashila trek is a blessing for first time trekkers particularly in the winters as the trails are covered in snow. This is an easily accessible trek and the last 60 km to the top of Chandrashila stands out with the feels it gives of climbing in the Himalayas.The trek begins with a drive to Sari village (from Haridwar). This is an all-season trek with easy to moderate trekking making it a good bet for any beginner. The Chandrashila trek is known for its scenic beauty. It passes through some beautiful forests and affords excellent views of the snow peaks. The trek even gives you the opportunity to visit the 1000-year-old Tungnath temple, which is the highest shrine of Lord Shiva. It is one of the panch-kedars and is believed to have been built by Arjuna himself. Chandrashila Peak is famous for its breathtaking 360-degree view of the Himalayan ranges. It is one of the few peaks that can also be climbed in the winter.

XIII
Kedarkantha Trek

Whether it's your 1st trek or your 10th - Kedarkantha appeases all. In winter, the trek is a delight with snow sheathing the grounds - the challenges also increase. With a trail that takes you through pine forests, oak trees and alpine meadows, and graces you with 360 degree views across the Garhwal and Kinnaur Himalayan regions - Kedarkantha is magic at a magician's peak.Kedarkantha, situated in the mountains of the tons river valley is a beautiful ridge peak; easily accessible anytime of the year. In the winters it snows in this valley and hence views from the summit are very rewarding. The trek goes through the Govind national park and gives you ample time to soak in the flora and fauna of this protected area. The summit lies at an altitude of 3850 m and reaching the top is very satisfying as you are rewarded with views of peaks like the Swargarohini, Banderpooch, Black and Ranglana.

XIV

Vasu-Ki-Tal Trek

Vasu ki Tal (Vasuki Lake) is a popular pilgrim and trekking destination situated at an altitude of 14, 200 ft, in the beautiful hill of kedarnath dham. The adjoining environment is wonderfully decked with high mountains and striking view of several peak of Himalayas. There blooms varied types of lively, colourful miniature flowers around the Vasuki Tal Lake. Brahma Kamal is well-known flower of this region. June to October is the best time to visit this enchanting spot is because when the weather is mild and pleasant. The self-evident lake offers an appealing view to the nature lover and provokes the poet hidden, even the most unromantic person falls in the trap. It is confined in by steep and rolling banks combined with lush green vegetation.

XV

Khatling Trek

The trek through Khatling Glacier is a very scenic one, and travels along the Bhilangana river valley with its foundation at the Khatling Glacier – the point of occurrence of river Bhilangna. A journey to Khatling Trek offers one outstanding and mighty views of some of the famous Himalayan giant peaks like Thalay Sagar, Jaonli, Kirtistambh & Bharte Khunta. One who goes camping on the green pastures of Chowki experiences fabulous natural beauty all around. Spectacular Khatling glacier, Rafting trip on the holy river, Ganges and the visit to the holy ghats (bathing area) & ashrams at Rishikesh are what travellers look for. And on the return voyage one can visit the Trijuginarayan temple believed to be the sacred spot where Lord Shiva and Goddess Parvati tied the knot.

XVI

Rupin Pass Trek

Starting from Dhaula in Uttarakhand and ending in Sangla in Himachal Pradesh, Rupin Pass is good hill-walking route. Rupin Pass is still untouched by the human population. It is located at an altitude of 15250 ft above sea level in the Dhauladhar ranges. The Pass consists of streams dug out of rock faces; wooden bridges cut through deep dark folds in the mountain, glaciers, icy slopes, and overextended snow fields. Traveling and climbing the Rupin Pass is rated as moderate to diffucult level. The trails follow the Rupin River all the way to the top guided by evergreen Deodarforests. While traveling through this path one can witness the change in culture from core Hinduism of Garhwal to mix of Hindu-Buddhism in the Sangla Valley.

Part B: Trekking in Kumaun

Most of the trails in Kumaon are relatively easy, with gradual ascents and descents over rolling hillas and through meadows (Bugials or Kharag). These trails offer breathtaking views of the high peaks such as Nanda Devi, Nanda Kot, Trisuli and Hardeol. Eastern Kumaon has recently been opened to foreign trekkers and the trails dominated by the Panchchuli group of peaks.

XVII
Pindari Glacier Trek

The Pindari Glacier path provides for a 90 km round-trip trek that most goers find comfortable to complete in six days. Trekking tours in India is incomplete if one has not trekked Pindari Glacier. It is often called the trekker's paradise. Certainly the most easily reachable glacier in the Kumaon region, the Pindari Glacier is picturesque. Pindari is a huge and steep glacier situated between the snow-capped Nanda Devi and Nanda Kot Mountains. The Pindari Glacier is a never-ending and a breadth taking experience. The valley is drained by the Pindar River that arises from the Pindari Glacier. The river, in its initial course, runs through sedimentary rocks and finally meets the Alakananda River. As one moves downhill from Phurkia up to Khati, one comes across numerous waterfalls, hanging valleys and tremendous rock faces. The entire trekking route is packed with natural beauty.

XVIII

Sunderdhunga Valley Trek

Sunderdhunga valley trek, a neighbor of the more famous Pindari and Kafni glacier treks is considered to be most beautiful trek. The name Sunderdhunga, literally suggests the valley of beautiful stones. The eminent glaciers of this valley are Maiktoli and Sukhram. Sunderdhunga trek follows river Sunderdhunga upstream from Khati until its origin, making way through thick forests home to many animals; remote, almost bordering on exotic, villages; glaciers and pristine alpine meadows.

XIX

Nanda Devi East BC and Milam Glacier Trek

The logest (27km) glacier in Garhwal / Kumaon and Uttar Pradesh Himalaya, fed by a number of ice tributaries from a backdrop dominated by Rishi Pahar (6992m), Hardeol (7161m), Trishul (7074m) and Nanda Gond (6315m).

Normally approached from the Munsiari roadhead 2133m, This is a wonderful trek in Kumaon Himalayas explores the fascinating Nanda Devi East Base Camp and astounding Milam Glacier. Kumaon Himalaya is an eye-catching area of the Indian Himalayas, bordering to the western end of Nepal and consists of the famous mountain of Nanda Devi (7,816m).

This part of the Himalaya fascinated many of the eminent explorers and mountaineers with the majority of them trying to open the clandestine of approaching Nanda Devi. This trek trails the Gori Ganga ravine to the village of Milam and then goes to the East Base Camp of elating Nanda Devi. The trail enters one of the most impressive mountain areas of the Himalayas nearby Nanda Devi and the adjoining peaks, this landscape combined with the mesmerizing historical background of the area make it one of the best treks in India.

XX

Ram Ganga-Namik Glacier Trek

Ram Ganga-Namik Glacier (Recently opened area with rough and tough walks) - Situated at the head of Ram Ganga Valley, between Gauri Ganga and Pindar valleys. This has been a restricted area; hence it has remained comparatively unknown to the trekking community. The approach to this glacier is a delightful excursion. Leti is the road head which can be reached from Bageshwar via Bharari and Samadhura. Leti (2050m) is a big village where porters can be hired.

XXI

Panchchuli base camp Trek

Panchchuli base camp (passes through a region bordering Nepal and Tibet) - Goes up to Darma Valley near the borders of Nepal and Tibet, an area of outstanding beauty and importance for anthropologists. The people are migratory by nature, and though living in a remote Himalayan Valley, are quite literate and far from being primitive. The train from Delhi to Pithoragarh Journeys 503km via Tanakpur. Via Almora is more picturesque, through Bageshwar, Chaukori and Berinag; the same distance. To proceed beyond Pithoragarh get an inner line permit from the District Magistrate there. Now take a bus for Dharchula (4h 30 journey), and, after changing, to Sobala is a roadhead and take off-point for this trek, though you can travel a few km further by jeep. Sobala to Panchchuli base camp is a pleasant walk of 28km. As the local people keep going up and down the valley, eating shops and accommodation are easily available.

XXII

Ralam Dhura Pass Trek

Ralam Dhura Pass (strenuous) - 5580 - A passage in the Panchchuli Range between Chaudhara (6510m) and Sui Tilla (6373m), from the Lassar Yankti Valley to Gauri Ganga Valley. From Pokhang (see above) in the Lassar Yankti, the route crosses two passes and negotiates three glaciers to reach Ralam village on the Ralam Gad, a tributary of the Gauri Ganga. At pokhang (3430m) ascend alogside the Ralam Yangti stream steeply though thorny shrubs and scree, past Ramta Dangsu to Gunda Dangsu (4200m), 4.5km from Pokhang and on the left side of Nipchikang Glacier.

HITCHHIKER'S GUIDE TO TREKKING IN UTTARAKHAND

Trekking is a popular adventure activity among the tourists. Trips to the mountains in India signify not only the natural beauty, but a source of spiritual guidance as well. The height and beauty of Indian Himalayas provide enthralling opportunities for trekking.

Trekking through different regions of the country gives an opportunity to the adventurers to gain a deep insight into the immaculate beauty of the regions and the bewitching flora and fauna as well. The mighty range of Himalayas present in India provides one of the amazing trekking experiences to visitors.

Uttarakhand is a 'paradise' for nature lover's and adventure sports like river rafting, trekking, paragliding, Corbett jungle Jeep safari, enthusiasts. The Gangotri area near the source of the Bhagirathi River is the most popular destination for trekkers and mountaineers. Hence the state has lot of potential for the trekking. If we go through the best ten trekking destination of the India, you will find the out of these ten 4 or 5 of Uttarakhand.

Some Interesting Notes On Trekking And Uttarakhand

Note: I

Uttarakhand's name is derived from the Sanskrit words *Uttara* meaning North, and meaning Land, simply means Northern Land. The name finds mention in early Hindu scriptures as the combined region of "Kedarkhand" (present day Garhwal) and "Manaskhand" (present day Kumaon). Uttarakhand was also the ancient Puranic term for the central stretch of the Indian Himalayas. Ancient rock paintings, rock shelters, paleolithic stone tools and megalithsprovide evidence that the mountains of the region have been inhabited since prehistoric times. There are also archaeological remains which show the existence of early Vedic practices in the area.

Archaeological evidence supports the existence of humans in the region since prehistoric times. Among the first major dynasties of Garhwal and Kumaon were the Kunindas in the 2nd century BC who practised an early form of Shaivism. Ashokan edicts at Kalsi show the early presence of Buddhism in this region. During the medieval period the region was consolidated under the Kumaon Kingdom and Garhwal Kingdom. By 1803 the region fell to the Gorkha Empire of Nepal and with the conclusion of the Anglo-Nepalese War in 1816 most of modern Uttarakhand was ceded to the British as part of the Treaty of Sugauli.

Although the erstwhile hill kingdoms of Garhwal and Kumaon were traditional rivals, the proximity of different neighbouring ethnic groups and the inseparable and complementary nature of their geography, economy, culture, language, and traditions created strong bonds between the two regions which further strengthened during the Uttarakhand movement for statehood in the 1990s.

The Pauravas, Kushanas, Kunindas, Guptas, Gurjara pratihara, Katyuris, Raikas, Palas, Chands, Parmars or Panwars, Sikhs, and theBritish have ruled Uttarakhand in turns. The region was originally settled by Kol people, an aboriginal people of the Austro-Asiatic physical type who were later joined by Indo-Aryan Khasas tribe hat arrived from the northwest by the Vedic period (1700–1100 BCE). At that time, present-day Uttarakhand also served as a habitat for Rishis and Sadhus. It is believed that the sage Vyasa scripted the Hindu epic *Mahabharata* in the state.

Among the first major dynasties of Garhwal and Kumaon were the Kunindas. By the medieval period, the region was consolidated under the Garhwal Kingdom in the west and the Kumaon Kingdom in the east. During this period, learning and new forms of painting (the Pahari School of art) developed. Modern-day Garhwal was likewise unified under the rule of Parmars who, along with many Brahmins and Rajputs, also arrived from the plains. In 1791 the expanding Gorkha Empire of Nepal overran Almora, the seat of the Kumaon Kingdom. In 1803 the Garhwal Kingdom also fell to the Gorkhas. With the conclusion of the Anglo-Nepalese War in 1816, the Garhwal Kingdom was re-established from a smaller region in Tehri, as the larger portion of Tehri, along with eastern Garhwal and Kumaon ceded to the British as part of the Treaty of Sugauli.

After India attained independence from the British, the Garhwal Kingdom was merged into the state of Uttar Pradesh, where Uttarakhand composed the Garhwal and Kumaon Divisions. Uttarakhand, which gained significant momentum in 1994, when demand for separate statehood achieved almost unanimous acceptance among both the local populace and national political parties.

The most notable incident during this period was the Rampur Tiraha firing case on the night of 1 October 1994, which led to a public uproar. On 24 September 1998, the Uttar Pradesh Legislative Assembly passed the Uttar Pradesh Reorganisation Bill, which began the process of creating a new state. Two years later the Parliament of India passed the Uttar Pradesh Reorganisation Act 2000, and thus, on 9 November 2000, Uttarakhand became the 27th state of the Republic of India.

Note: II

Uttarakhand implies the terrain and the landforms present within its territory. Nestled amid the Himalayas, the topography of Uttarakhand offers a wide range of landforms form hills and peak to cliffs and ridges.The topography of Uttarakhand boasts of many rich forests, glaciers, mountains peaks, and beautiful network of the mighty rivers. In fact, the hills and mountains present in the territory of Kumaoni-Garhwal is said to be the 'Abode of Gods and Goddesses'.

Uttarakhand is known for its natural beauty of the Himalayas, the Bhabhar and the Terai. On 9 November 2000, this 27th state of the Republic of India was carved out of the Himalayan and adjoining north-western districts of Uttar Pradesh. It borders the Tibet Autonomous Region on the north; the Mahakali Zone of the Far-Western Region, Nepal on the east; and the Indian states of Uttar Pradesh to the south and Himachal Pradesh to the northwest. The state is divided into two divisions, Garhwal and Kumaon, with a total of 13 districts.

Uttarakhand has a great diversity of flora and fauna. It has a recorded forest area of 34651 km2 which constitutes 65% of the total area of the state. Uttarakhand is home to rare species of plants and animals, many of which are protected by sanctuaries and reserves a number of plant species in the valley is internationally threatened, including several that have not been recorded from elsewhere in Uttarakhand. Rajaji National Park in Haridwar District and Govind Pashu Vihar National Park and Sanctuary and Gangotri National Park in Uttarkashi District are some other protected areas in the state.

The state is full with the natural resources.

In the floral world the Evergreen oaks, rhododendrons, and conifers predominate in the hills. Shorea robusta (sal), silk cotton tree (Bombax ciliata), Dalbergia sissoo, Mallotus philippensis, Acacia catechu, Bauhinia racemosa, and Bauhinia variegata (camel's foot tree) are some of the other trees of the region. Albizia chinensis, the sweet sticky flowers of which are favoured by sloth bears, are also part of the region's flora. The park has many species of medicinal plants including Dactylorhiza hatagirea, Picrorhiza kurroa.

In the fauna world, Leopards are found in areas which are abundant in hills but may also venture into the lowland jungles. Smaller felines include the jungle cat, fishing cat, and leopard cat. Other mammals include four kinds of deer (barking, sambar, hog and and chital) sloth and Himalayan black bears, Indian grey mongooses, otters, yellow-throated martens, bharal (goat-antelopes), Indian pangolins and langur and rhesus monkeys. In the summer, elephants can be seen in herds of several hundred. Marsh crocodiles (Crocodylus palustris), Gharials (Gavialis gangeticus) and other reptiles are also found in the region.

Local crocodiles were saved from extinction by captive breeding programs and subsequently re-released into the Ramganga River. Several freshwater terrapins and turtles like the Indian sawback turtle (Kachuga tecta), Brahminy river turtle (Hardella thurgii), and Ganges softshell turtle(Trionyx gangeticus) are found in the rivers. Butterflies and birds of the region include red Helen (Papilio helenus), the great eggfly (Hypolimnos bolina), common tiger (Danaus genutia), pale wanderer (Pareronia avatar avatar), Jungle Babbler, Tawny – bellied Babbler, Great Slaty Woodpecker, Red – breasted Parakeet, Orange – Breasted Green Pigeon and Chestnut – winged Cuckoo.

Note: III

Uttarakhand is endowed with a unique and diverse range of biodiversity. From the snowbound peaks of the Himalayas to the moist Alpine scrub, sub Alpine forests, dry - temperate and moist- temperate forests to moist deciduous forests, the state possesses a wide biodiversity that in return nurtures a large multiplicity of floral and faunal forms.

Uttarakhand comprises of 13 districts spreading over an area of 51,082 sq km, floristically, it falls under the west Himalayan Biogeography zone and it is well-known for floral diversity similar to any other Himalayan region in the country with an estimated 4,000 species of flowering plants having great economic medicinal, aromatic and artistic value. The endemic plant wealth of Uttarakhand is worth mentioning as it ultimately forms part of the National heritage. Uttarakhand Himalayas have about 116 species asindigenous group. Are naria ferruginea; Chimonobambusa jaunsarensis, Gentian tetrasepala, G. saginoides, Meeboldia solenoids, Microschoenus duthiei,

Trachycarpus takil, Poa rhadina, etc are some such species.

A decade long study by Prof. C.P. Kala concluded that the Valley of Flowers is endowed with 520 species of higher plants (angiosperms, gymnosperms and pteridophytes), of these 498 are flowering plants. The park has many species of medicinal plants including Dactylorhiza hatagirea, Picrorhiza kurroa, Aconitum violaceum, Polygonatum multiflorum, Fritillaria roylei, and Podophyllum hexandrum.

The state is home to nearly 4048 species of Angiosperms and Gymnosperms belonging to 1198 genera under 192 families. Of these nearly 116 species are specific to Uttarakhand i.e. their geographical distribution is limited to the boundaries of the state. 161 species of flora found in Uttarakhand are recognized as rare or threatened under the categorization of the International Union for Conservation of Nature (IUCN). Out of the 223 species of Orchids reported from the North Western Himalayas, over 150 have been reported from the State.

This precious natural wealth is our common heritage. In order to conserve this heritage, the state has declared twelve areas as 'Protected' including 6 National Parks and six Wildlife Sanctuaries. Nearly 65% of the geographical area of the State is under forest cover, of which over 12% comes under the Protected Area network. This exceeds the national average by a fair margin and is a reflection of the state's commitment to conservation. The Corbett National Park, established in 1936 is the first National Park of the Asian mainland. The Nandadevi Biosphere Reserve, established under the "Man and biosphere" programme of UNESCO has the honour of being Uttarakhand's only and the country's second Biosphere Reserve. This biodiversity wealth is the pride of Uttarakhand.

Besides, many plant species new to science have been added from different parts of Uttarakhand. Some such species are Anemone raui, Arenaria curvifolia, Carex nandadviensis, List era nandadeviensis, Saussurea sudhanshui, Euphorbia sharmae, Androsace garhwalicum, etc. More interesting to note is the presence of one of the smallest flowering plants Arceuthobium minutissimum, parasitising over Pinus gerardiana (Chilgoza) and the tallest plant of Asia, the Pinus roxburghii, in Uttarkashi district.

The sacred Mulberry, Morus serrata, said to have been planted by the Adi Shankaracharya at Joshimath, the tree fern Cyathea spinulosa, the gigantic Aesculus indica on way to Panwali, the tall Shore a Robusta (Raja Sal) near Byasi are some other curiosities of the area. The narrative of the plant wealth of Uttarakhand will not be complete unless a mentioned about the sacred plants commonly used in worship in "The Abode of Gods". Besides, the earlier mentioned "Brahmakamal", Zanthoxylum armatum (Timur), Prunus puddum (Panya), Skimmia laureola, Primula denticulata, and Artemisia nilagirica, Eagle marvelous etc. are offered to deities.

Note: IV

Uttarakhand has a multiethnic population spread across two geo-cultural regions: the Gahrwal, and the Kumaon. A large portion of the population is Rajput (various clans of landowning rulers and their descendants)—including members of the native Garhwali, Kumaoni and Gujjar communities, as well as a number of immigrants.

Approximately one-fifth of the population belongs to the Scheduled Castes (an official term for the lower castes in the traditional Hindu caste system).

Scheduled Tribes (an official term for natives outside the Indian social system), such as the Raji, who live near the border with Nepal, constitute less than 3 percent of the population.

More than four-fifths of Uttarakhand's residents are Hindus. Approx 85% are Hindus. According to a 2007 study, Uttarakhand has the highest percentage of Brahmins of any state in India, with approximately 20% of the population being Brahmin. Muslims, Sikhs, Christians, Buddhists, and Jains make up the remaining population with the Muslims being the largest minority. "In those lovely valleys there is still the romance and poetry of life: each tree has its god, each bush its spirit" – So wrote the 19th century British anthropologist and surveyor Charles A. Sherring, describing a fair part of Uttarakhand, in his great research 'Western Tibet and British Borderland'.

All the local traditions of the state are determinedly attached to nature and its bounty. No legends or myths are complete without nature, seasons or the Himalayas being integral part of them. The people spare no opportunity to celebrate this bountiful natural, social and religious diversity. Collective celebrations become the order of the day – the many fairs and festivals bear testimony to this. These fairs have now become remarkable stages for all sort of uncluttered social, cultural and economic exchange. Visitors from far and wide are drawn to these events in multitudes.

The state offers journey-options to both – the religious and the spiritual. There are a number of religious events attached to River Ganga - the holiest of all the rivers. Daily aartis performed every evening at the banks of the Mother-River in Haridwar and Rishikesh present a memorable sight to behold when the star studded sky seems to be reflecting the serene waters of the river upon the surface of which float countless diyas offered to the goddess. The Kumbh Mela that is held every twelve years witnesses some of the largest gatherings of devotees to be seen anywhere in the whole world.

Overwhelming natural panoramas accompany the pilgrims taking part in the Nanda Devi Raj Jaat and Kailash Mansarovar Yatras. The shrines of Hemkund Sahib and Nanakmatta Sahib are visited by thousands of Sikh devotees while a symbol of national integration - the Dargaah at Piran Kaliyar Sharif, holds a significant religious rank for Muslims and people from other faiths alike.

Several indigenous tribes and communities flourish in this state today maintaining their distinct cultural heritage and traditions. The several fairs and festivals celebrated by the tribes such as Bhotias (Shaukas), Tharus, Buxas and Jaunsaris are opportunity for the locals and the visitors to witness these events and keep the traditional modes of life and art alive apart from providing them the recognition they so strongly deserve.

Legends, myths and anecdotes galore in the state of Uttarakhand which has in turn been bestowed by the richest, holy rivers and the most esteemed mountains. Series of legends and tales are intricately woven around the sacred shrines, temples and rivers by simple hearted, god-fearing people that simultaneously reflect the socio-cultural diversity of the state.

Note: V

Mountaineering and rock climbing is getting popularity day by day. Before starting its famous destination in

Uttarkahand we must go to its history. Historically, many cultures have harbored superstitions about mountains, which they often regarded as sacred due to their proximity with heaven, such as Mount Olympus for the Ancient Greeks. In 1573 Francesco De Marchi and Francesco Di Domenico ascended Corno Grande, the highest peak in the Apennine Mountains. During the Enlightenment, as a product of the new spirit of curiosity for the natural world, many mountain summits were surmounted for the first time. Richard Pococke and William Windham made a historic visit to Chamonix in 1741. In 1760, the Swiss scientist, Horace-Bénédict de Saussure, offered a reward for the first person to ascend Mont Blanc in France, which was claimed in 1786.

By the early 19th century many of the alpine peaks were reached; the Grossglockner in 1800, the Ortler in 1804, the Jungfrau in 1811, the Finsteraarhorn in 1812, and the Breithorn in 1813. The beginning of mountaineering as a systematic sport is generally dated to the ascent of the Wetterhorn in 1854 by Sir Alfred Wills who made mountaineering fashionable, especially in Britain. This inaugurated what became known as the Golden age of alpinism, with the first mountaineering club - the Alpine Club - being founded in 1857.Prominent figures of the period include Lord Francis Douglas, Florence Crauford Grove,Charles Hudson, E. S. Kennedy, William Mathews, A. W. Moore, Leslie Stephen, Francis Fox Tuckett, John Tyndall, Horace Walker and Edward Whymper. Well-known guides of the era include Christian Almer, Jakob Anderegg, Melchior Anderegg, J. J. Bennen, Michel Croz, and Johannes Zumtaugwald.

In the early years of the "golden age", scientific pursuits were intermixed with the sport, such as by the physicist

John Tyndall. In the later years of the "golden age", it shifted to a more competitive orientation as pure sportsmen came to dominate the London-basedAlpine Club and alpine mountaineering overall.One of the most dramatic events was the spectacular first ascent of the Matterhorn in 1865, by a party led by the English illustrator, Edward Whymper - four of the party members fell to their deaths. This ascent is generally regarded as marking the end of the mountaineering golden age. By this point the sport of mountaineering had largely reached its modern form, with a body of professional guides, equipment and fixed guidelines.

Focus shifted toward the exploration of other ranges such as the Pyrenees and the Caucasus Mountains; the latter owed much to the initiative of D. W. Freshfield who was the first man to conquer the summit of Mount Kazbek. Most of its great peaks were successfully conquered by the late 1880s. Mountaineering in the Americas became popular in the 1800s. In North America, Pikes Peak(14,410 ft (4,390 m)) in the Colorado Rockies, was first climbed by Edwin James and two others in 1820.

Though lower than Pikes Peak, the heavily glaciated Fremont Peak (13,745 ft (4,189 m)) in Wyoming was thought to be the tallest mountain in the Rockies when it was first climbed by John C. Frémont and two others in 1842. Pico de Orizaba (18,491 ft (5,636 m)), the tallest peak in Mexico and third tallest in North America, was first summited by U.S. military personnel which included William F. Raynolds and a half dozen other climbers in 1848. Heavily glaciated and more technical climbs in North American were not achieved until the late 19th and early 20th centuries. In 1897, Mount Saint Elias (18,008 ft (5,489 m)) on the Alaska-Yukon border was summited by the Duke of the Abruzzi and party.

But it was not until 1913 that Mount Mckinley (20,237 ft (6,168 m)), the tallest peak in North America, was successfully climbed. Mount Logan (19,551 ft (5,959 m)), the tallest peak in Canada, was first summitted by a half dozen climbers in 1925 in an expedition that took more than two months.

The last and greatest mountain range was the Himalayas in Central Asia. They had initially been surveyed by the British Empire for military and strategic reasons. In 1892 Sir William Martin Conway explored the Karakoram Himalayas, and climbed a peak of 23,000 ft (7,000 m) In 1895 Albert F. Mummery died while attempting Nanga Parbat, while in 1899 D. W. Freshfield took an expedition to the snowy regions of Sikkim. In 1899, 1903, 1906 and 1908 Mrs Fannie Bullock Workman made ascents in the Himalayas, including one of the Nun Kun peaks (23,300 ft).

A number of Gurkha sepoys were trained as expert mountaineers by Charles G. Bruce, and a good deal of exploration was accomplished by them.

Note: VI

Bordered by Tibet in the north, Nepal in the east, Himachal Pradesh in the west and the Gangetic plains in the south, Uttarakhand, the land of spirituality seems to be a jewel on the crown of Indian Territory. Being the originating point of significant Indian rivers, Uttarakhand is the abode of some of the best hill stations in north India. While the winter season can offer you the best views of snow packed mountain ranges, the same ranges can be the comfort zones in the scorching summer.

From thrilling mountain climbing to relaxing leisure walk, each single activity is delightful and worthy to time spending. Hill stations are visited by honeymooners to spend romantic time together, corporate people to take a break, traveller to enjoy the beauteousness of nature, family to enjoy vacation and creative persons to enhance their creativity level with fresh ideas. An Uttarakhand Hill station is a compilation of several popular destinations of Uttarakhand which are popular with the masses and have frequented visitors. Don't search reasons for planning a holiday in the hill stations of Uttarakhand and simply pack your bags to take pleasure in the pristine scenery of the Himalayas.

Uttarakhand is a 'paradise' for nature lovers and adventure sports like river rafting, trekking, paragliding, Corbett jungle Jeep safari, enthusiasts. Mussoorie, the 'Queen of Hills'; Nainital, Almora, Ranikhet, Pithoragarh, Pauri and Munsiyari are just few highlights for the nature lovers.

For adventure and excitement, one may choose Mountaineering (Bhagirathi, Chowkhamba, Nanda Devi Kamet, Pindari, Sahastrataal, Milam, Kafni, Khatling, Gaumukh), Trekking, Skiing (Auli, Dayara Bugyal, Munsiyari, Mundali), Skating, Water Sports like rafting, boating and angling and Aero Sports like Hand Gliding, Paragliding (Pithoragarh, Jolly Grant, Pauri).Trekking adventure in the Uttarakhand's enchanting Himalayas have always been appealing the trekking lovers and adventure sports enthusiasts. Explore Valley of Flowers, Chopta and the beauty of Kumaon and Garhwal Himalayas.

AUTHOR

Dr Anshumali Pandey, PhD, Author

Dr. Anshumali Pandey, is a renowned & reliable name in the field of Education, Hospitality, Tourism and Tribal Food. He is a Teacher and Chef by profession, and also an Author, a Business Auditor, and an avid culinary traveller to the Indian Sub continental hinterlands. Dr. Anshumali Pandey is a Hospitality Educator (PhD) who specialises in Higher Education, Office Administration, Pay roll, HR, Labour Laws, Audit, and Procurement & Tender Process. He is an Author with 41 Publications consisting of 26 Books.

The books written by Dr Anshumali Pandey are essentially a banquet arising from an experience of over

25 years of Professional life and have boiled down to crisp and accurate writing on his favourite subjects. Hospitality Sector champion requires to be a specialist in many fields and Dr Pandey is one of them. His knowledge is evident from the spectrum of subjects which he has chosen for his books so far, which ranges from being a specialist chef, to Master of Human resources, to Education and to love for children, and topped with Spirituality.

Books written by the Author are –

1. Theory of Indian Cookery
2. Beauty and Irony of Silvassa Tourism
3. A Short Indian Food Story
4. Be Your Own Guide to Indian Cuisine
5. Cookery Fundamentals
6. History of Indian Food
7. The Great Indian Story Book for Children
8. Personal Budget: Easy Work Book
9. Online Classes Log Book
10. Dictionary Making Work Book for School Children
11. The Lazy Bed
12. Hindu Dharm (In Hindi Language)
13. Where is my coffee?
14. Your First Job is Never your Last (Volume 1)
15. You are Almost There (Quick Fix Resume and Interview Hacks)
16. Working for the Enemy? - A lesson in Career Management
17. Public Speaking for the Young
18. A Date With Coffee
19. How to be The Best Hotel Front Office Employee
20. Diploma in Food Production, The complete Syllabus
21. Diploma in F&B Service, The Complete Syllabus

22. Diploma in Front Office, The Complete Syllabus
23. The Time to Speak is Now
24. Munshi Premchand (Short Stories in English)
25. The Housekeeping Department, Text Book
26. Hitchhiker's Guide to Trekking in Uttarakhand

Connect with me: anshumali.pandey@gmail.com
https://notionpress.com/author/337004

Please scan this QR Code to connect with the Author Online.

9 798886 293210

Printed by Libri Plureos GmbH in Hamburg,
Germany